CONCORD BRANCH LIBRARY
2900 SALVIO STREET
CONCORD, CALIFORNIA 94519

CONCORD

MAY 0 1 2007

D1459734

CONCORD BRANCH LIBRARY
2900 SALVIO STREET
CONCORD, CALIFORNIA 94519

MAY 0 1 2007

Santa Knows

BY
Cynthia & Greg
Leitich Smith

WITHDRAWN

CONTRA COSTA COUNTY LIBRARY

ILLUSTRATED
BY
Steve
Björkman

DUTTON
CHILDREN'S
BOOKS

Santa Stinks!

3 1901 03998 2378

For Caroline Smith and in memory of Harry "Bud" Smith.

With thanks to Steve Björkman, Anne Bustard, Tim Crow,
Ginger Knowlton, Uma Krishnaswami, Mark McVeigh,
and Sean Petrie.

Merry Christmas from Cynthia and Greg!
—C & GLS

———————————————

For Kristi with love
—SB

DUTTON CHILDREN'S BOOKS. A division of Penguin Young Readers Group
Published by the Penguin Group • Penguin Group (USA) Inc., 375 Hudson Street, New York, New York 10014, U.S.A. • Penguin Group (Canada), 90 Eglinton Avenue
East, Suite 700, Toronto, Ontario, Canada M4P 2Y3 (a division of Pearson Penguin Canada Inc.) • Penguin Books Ltd, 80 Strand, London WC2R 0RL, England •
Penguin Ireland, 25 St Stephen's Green, Dublin 2, Ireland (a division of Penguin Books Ltd) • Penguin Group (Australia), 250 Camberwell Road, Camberwell,
Victoria 3124, Australia (a division of Pearson Australia Group Pty Ltd) • Penguin Books India Pvt Ltd, 11 Community Centre, Panchsheel Park, New Delhi -
110 017, India • Penguin Group (NZ), Cnr Airborne and Rosedale Roads, Albany, Auckland 1310, New Zealand (a division of Pearson New Zealand Ltd) • Penguin
Books (South Africa) (Pty) Ltd, 24 Sturdee Avenue, Rosebank, Johannesburg 2196, South Africa • Penguin Books Ltd, Registered Offices: 80 Strand, London
WC2R 0RL, England

Text copyright © 2006 by Cynthia and Greg Leitich Smith
Illustrations copyright © 2006 by Steve Björkman

All rights reserved.

Library of Congress Cataloging-in-Publication Data

Smith, Cynthia Leitich.
Santa knows / by Cynthia and Greg Leitich Smith ; illustrations by
Steve Björkman. — 1st ed.
p. cm.
Summary: Armed with the facts, young Alfie sets out to prove to the world that Santa Claus does not exist, but no one pays attention,
especially his sister Noelle, whose only request of the man in red is a nicer big brother.
ISBN 0-525-47757-8 (alk. paper)
[1. Santa Claus—Fiction. 2. Brothers and sisters—Fiction.
3. Behavior—Fiction. 4. Belief and doubt—Fiction. 5. Christmas —Fiction.]
I. Smith, Greg Leitich. II. Björkman, Steve, ill.
III. Title.
PZ7.S64464San 2006
[E]—dc22   2005036723

Published in the United States by Dutton Children's Books, a division of Penguin Young Readers Group
345 Hudson Street, New York, New York 10014
www.penguin.com/youngreaders

Designed by Irene Vandervoort

Manufactured in China   First Edition

1 3 5 7 9 10 8 6 4 2

lfie F. Snorklepuss yanked his little sister's
Christmas stocking from the fireplace mantel.

"Hey!" Noelle exclaimed. "Give *that* back!"

"There's no such thing as Santa Claus," Alfie said. "So why bother?"

"I believe," Noelle whispered, "and you should, *too!*"

But Alfie had decided *that* believing in Santa Claus was silly. "I'll prove it!" he said. "I'll prove *there* is no Santa Claus!"

So Alfie went to the library.

He read books about flying. He read books about reindeer.

He read books about flying reindeer.

He read every book he could find about Santa Claus, elves, Christmas Eve, and the North Pole. He studied the globe. He checked to see if any jet companies made sleighs.

"That's it!" he said finally, closing the last book. "Even at the speed of light, with changing time zones and different calendars, there is no way anyone could deliver kajillions of pounds of gifts to hundreds of millions of kids all in one night. There. Is. No. Santa Claus!"

"Think about the facts!"
he scolded the kids at school.

No one is that fast,
he wrote in a letter to the editor.

"The weight alone would cripple
an old fat man," he told the radio DJ.

"Besides, have you ever seen a real live elf?" he asked the TV audience.

"Wake up and smell the cookies!" he posted on the World Wide Web. "At least they're for real."

But no one paid attention to Alfie.

Not the kids at school or the ones who read the newspaper or those who listened to the radio or watched TV or surfed the Web. Especially not his sister, Noelle.

When Alfie saw Noelle hang her stocking back on the mantel, he tore it off again and said, "Santa Claus *this*, Santa Claus *that!* Face it! He's nothing but a fairy tale!"

"Think what you want, Alfie F. Snorklepuss," Noelle replied. "Santa Claus believes in people who believe in him."

On Christmas Eve, Noelle wrote her letter to Santa:

December 24

Dear Santa:

All I want for Christmas is a nicer big brother.

XOXO,

J. Noelle Snorklepuss

"Bah!" Alfie sneered.

But Noelle ignored him and dropped her letter in the mailbox.

That night, Alfie F. Snorklepuss pretended to sleep, but really, he was waiting up for Santa to not arrive. "Humbug!" he muttered, closing his eyes.

He awoke to a clatter on the roof.

"Nah, couldn't be," Alfie mumbled, looking toward the twinkling tree.

"Ho, ho, ho!" he heard from the fireplace. "Merry Christmas!"

"No way!" Alfie insisted. But as he rose to look, suddenly there appeared in front of him the Jolly Old Elf himself.

"What's the matter?" Santa said merrily. "Reindeer got your tongue?"

"But, but, but—" Alfie sputtered. "The speed! The time! The weight! Impossible!"

"Permit me to explain, Alfred Franklin Snorklepuss,"
Santa began with a twinkle in his eye. "My sleigh stops
time around me so I can deliver gifts to every good little boy
and girl by Christmas morning."

"Stops time?" Alfie squeaked.

"My bag," Santa went on, "is a gateway to my workshop. It
goes with me around the world."

Alfie paused. "I don't think so!"

"It's elf science and technology," Santa explained. "Ho, ho,
ho!"

Alfie scowled, shaking his head.

"Oh, here then," Santa sighed. "It's much easier to show you." With that, he tossed Alfie into his bag. "Don't touch anything!" Santa yelled after him.

A second later, Alfie found himself on a conveyor belt.

"Where am I?" he asked, looking around. "I—I don't believe it! Santa's Workshop!"

"Look!" exclaimed a worker elf. "A boy doll."

"How realistic!" a second elf said. "The elves in plastics know their stuff."

"Hmm," said another. "It has an unpleasant expression."

"Still," replied their supervisor, "Santa must've put in the order for a reason."

"Wait!" Alfie begged as the belt whizzed him away. "I'm not a toy!"

A packaging elf ordered, "Grab a big box!"

"Stop!" Alfie said. "I need airholes!"

"It talks," noted an assistant. "What a snazzy doll!"

"Just do what it says," his coworker answered.

"Who gets this one?" asked a clerk.

"Check the paperwork," the distribution elf suggested.

"Let's worry about it later," said their boss. "It's cocoa-break time!"

"Hey, elfin guys?" Alfie called as they strolled away. "Guys? Anybody? Help!"

Alfie was cold.

Alfie was hungry.

Alfie was lonely.

And Alfie was just a little scared.

So, he thought. There really is a Santa Claus. Noelle was right all along. Alfie wished he'd been nicer to her.

He wished he hadn't said all those mean things about Santa Claus.

"Santa," he said in a small, sad voice, "if you can hear me, I believe in you. I believe in elf science and technology, too. What's more, I... I believe I can be a nice boy. A nicer big brother. If you'll just give me another chance, I promise I'll be the nicest big brother in the world."

Alfie fell asleep waiting for an answer.

The following morning, Noelle raced to see what was under the tree.

It was a big box with a big bow. And airholes.

The tag read:

FOR NOELLE

MERRY CHRISTMAS!

FROM SANTA

"Where's Alfie?" Mama asked.

"Probably still asleep," Daddy said.

That's when they all heard a snore coming from Noelle's present. "Zzzzzz…"

for Noelle
Merry Christmas!
from Santa

She tugged the ribbon loose and the box fell open, revealing Alfie, who was still snoring away. She woke up Alfie, who hugged Mama and Daddy and Noelle, too.

"From now on," Alfie promised, "I'm going to be a nicer big brother."

"I know," Noelle answered. "I believe in you!"